Join the Little Golden
Billion Golden Memories
Celebration

$100,000 in prizes!

2 GRAND PRIZES:
7-day Cruise to the Caribbean for a family of 4 (two adults and two children) including round-trip airfare and stateroom accommodations plus $2,000 cash

6 FIRST PRIZES:
Zenith® Home Video Entertainment Center (TV, VCR, Video Camcorder)

12 SECOND PRIZES:
Zenith® Video Cassette Recorder **plus** 12 Golden Book Video® Cassettes

40 THIRD PRIZES:
Zenith® 9" DeLights Color TV

500 FOURTH PRIZES:
Set of 8 Golden Junior Classic™ Storybooks

——— PLUS ———

7,000 BONUS PRIZES*:
$4.95 Golden® Storybook

* Bonus prize for the first 7,000 consumers to share their favorite memory of Little Golden Books with us.

TO ENTER:
Just complete the official entry form** found in each specially marked Little Golden Book, First Little Golden Book® and Big Little Golden Book® displaying the "BILLION GOLDEN® MEMORIES" symbol on its cover.

** NO PURCHASE NECESSARY TO ENTER. See sweepstakes rule #2 for alternate entry requirements.

BONUS!
Favorite Golden® Memories Offer
turn page for details

turn page for details

Official Entry Form	Submit by December 31, 1987

Join the Little Golden Books®
Billion Golden Memories Celebration

Send this completed form to:

BILLION GOLDEN MEMORIES CELEBRATION
Dept. 9045 • Wheeling, IL 60090

Please tell us the title of your favorite Little Golden Book®:

_____
(PLEASE PRINT OR TYPE)

Name: _____

Address: _____

City: _____ State: _____ Zip: _____

Only One Entry Per Envelope. Enter as often as you wish, but use only official entry forms or alternate entry forms. Mechanically reproduced entries and photocopies are not permitted. Each entry must be sent separately via First Class mail in a #10 letter size envelope and be received no later than December 31, 1987. Offer good only in U.S.A.

Billion Golden® Memories Celebration

OFFICIAL RULES

NO PURCHASE NECESSARY TO ENTER

1. **TO ENTER,** simply write the title of your favorite LITTLE GOLDEN BOOK® on the entry certificate from the inside first page of each selected Little Golden Book, First Little Golden Book® or Big Little Golden Book® displaying the special "BILLION GOLDEN® MEMORIES" symbol on its cover. Then, complete your official entry form (hand-print or type) and mail it to:

   BILLION GOLDEN MEMORIES CELEBRATION
   Dept. 9045, Wheeling, IL 60090

2. **TO RECEIVE AN ALTERNATE ENTRY FORM WITHOUT MAKING A PURCHASE,** simply send a self-addressed #10 letter size stamped envelope by November 1, 1987 to:

   BILLION GOLDEN MEMORIES CELEBRATION
   ALTERNATE ENTRY FORM
   P.O. Box 1410, Wheeling, IL 60090

   Alternate entry forms are only available while *supplies last.* One official alternate entry form will be sent per envelope. Residents of the states of Washington and Vermont need not include postage.

3. Enter as often as you wish, but use only official entry forms or alternate entry forms. Mechanically reproduced entries and photocopies are not permitted. *Each* entry must be sent separately via First Class mail in a #10 letter size envelope and must be received *no later than December 31, 1987.* Mail each entry to:

   BILLION GOLDEN MEMORIES CELEBRATION
   Dept. 9045, Wheeling, IL 60090

4. Prizes to be awarded include **2 GRAND PRIZES:** 7-day Cruise to the Caribbean for a family of 4 (two adults and two children) including round trip airfare via coach or special fare, double occupancy stateroom accommodations (Trip *must* be taken before November 15,1988) plus $2,000 cash, worth approximately $6,000* each; **6 FIRST PRIZES:** Zenith® Home Video Entertainment Center (25" Stereo Color TV, VCR, Video Camcorder) valued at $2,504* each; **12 SECOND PRIZES:** Zenith® Video Cassette Recorder plus 12 Golden Book Video® Cassettes worth $629* each; **40 THIRD PRIZES:** Zenith® 9" DeLights Television worth $259* each; **500 FOURTH PRIZES:** Set of 8 Golden Junior Classic™ storybooks valued at $40* per set. **7,000 BONUS PRIZES:** Golden® Story Book worth $4.95* each. Total prizes are valued at approximately $100,000*. Merchandise prize deliveries are limited to the U.S.
   *Market value as of November, 1986.

5. *The first 7,000 consumers to hand-print or type their name, address, city, state, zip code and telephone number (including area code) along with their fondest memory of Little Golden Books on a sheet of 8½" x 11" paper will receive a FREE book from Western Publishing Company, Inc. worth at least $4.95 each. Memories must be a minimum of 25 words.*

   Each memory must be sent in a separate envelope to:
   MY FAVORITE MEMORY OF LITTLE GOLDEN BOOKS
   P.O. Box 1410, Wheeling, IL 60090
   Only one bonus prize per name, address or household. All entries become the property of Western Publishing Company, Inc. By submitting your fondest memory of Little Golden Books, you consent to the use of your submission, name and likeness for advertising, promotion, public relations or trade purposes with no additional compensation. Do not include your official or alternate sweepstakes entry form with this submission.

6. Sweepstakes begins March 1, 1987 or whenever first entry is received and ends December 31, 1987. Sponsor is not responsible for late, lost, misdirected, mutilated or stolen entries via mail. Entries will be randomly selected by David Kessler & Associates, Inc., an independent judging agency whose decisions are final on all matters relating to this sweepstakes. Drawing to be held during the week of January 25, 1988. All prizes will be awarded. Odds of winning based on number of entries received. Only one prize per household. Prizes are non-transferable and no substitutions are allowed. Travel arrangements and accommodations are by sponsor's choice. Taxes on each prize are the sole responsibility of the respective winners. Winners will be notified by March 1, 1988. The winners will be notified by mail and may be required to sign and return an affidavit of eligibility and release from liability within thirty (30) days of notification. Alternate winners will be selected in the event of non-compliance or the return of any undeliverable prize or notification of prize award.

7. Sweepstakes open to all residents of the U.S. Employees and their immediate family members of Western Publishing Company, Inc., its affiliates, participating retailers, agencies, contractors associated with this sweepstakes and David Kessler and Associates, Inc., are not eligible. All prizes will be awarded to a parent or legal guardian if the winner is a minor. By entering, winners consent to the use of their names and likenesses for advertising, promotion, public relations or trade purposes with no additional compensation. If a prize is not generally available at the end of the contest, a substitution of equal or greater value will be made. Void where prohibited by law and subject to all Federal, state and local regulations.

8. For a list of major winners, send a self-addressed #10 letter size stamped envelope to:
   BILLION GOLDEN MEMORIES CELEBRATION
   WINNERS LIST
   P.O. Box 1410, Wheeling, IL 60090
   Do not include request for the winner's list with your sweepstakes entry.

   Sponsor: Western Publishing Company, Inc.
   Racine, Wisconsin 53404
   © 1987 Western Publishing Company, Inc.

The Shy Little Kitten

story by CATHLEEN SCHURR
pictures by GUSTAF TENGGREN

A GOLDEN BOOK • NEW YORK

Western Publishing Company, Inc., Racine, Wisconsin 53404

Way up in the hayloft of an old red barn lived a mother cat and her new baby kittens. There were five bold and frisky little roly-poly black and white kittens, and *one* little striped kitten who was very, very shy.

One day, the five bold little roly-poly black
and white kittens and the one little roly-poly
striped kitten who was very, very shy all sat
down and washed their faces and paws with

busy little red tongues. They smoothed down
their soft baby fur and stroked their whiskers
and followed their mother down the ladder
from the hayloft—jump, jump, jump!

Then off they marched, straight out of the cool, dark barn, into the warm sunshine. How soft the grass felt under their paws! The five bold and frisky little kittens rolled over in the grass and kicked up their heels with joy.

But the shy little striped kitten just stood off
by herself at the very end of the line.

That was how she happened to see the earth
push up in a little mound right in front of her.
Then—*pop!*—up came a pointed little nose.
The nose belonged to a chubby mole.

"Good morning!" said the mole, as friendly

as you please. "Won't you come for a walk with me?"

"Oh," said the shy little kitten. She looked shyly over her shoulder.

But the mother cat and her five bold and frisky kittens had disappeared from sight.

So the shy little kitten went walking with the chubby mole. Soon they met a speckled frog sitting near the pond.

"My, what big eyes he has!" whispered the shy little kitten. But the frog had sharp ears, too.

He chuckled. "My mouth is much bigger. Look!" And the frog opened his great cave of a mouth.

The mole and the kitten laughed and laughed until their sides ached.

When the kitten stopped laughing and looked around, the frog had vanished. On the pond, ripples spread out in great silver circles.

"I really should be getting back to my mother and the others," said the shy little kitten, "but I don't know where to find them."

"I'll show you," said a strange voice. And out of the bushes bounded a shaggy black puppy.

"Oh, thank you," said the shy kitten. "Good-bye, mole."

So off they went together, the shy kitten and the shaggy puppy dog. The little kitten, of course, kept her eyes shyly on the ground.

But the shaggy puppy stopped to bark,
"Woof, woof," at a red squirrel in a tree. He
was full of mischief.

"Chee, chee, chee," the squirrel chattered
back. And she dropped a hickory nut right on
the puppy's nose. She was very brave.

"Wow, wow, wow," barked the mischievous
puppy, and off they went toward the farm.
Soon they came bounding out of the woods,
and there before them stretched the farmyard.

"Here we are," said the shaggy puppy dog. So down the hillside they raced, across the bridge above the brook, and straight on into the farmyard.

In the middle of the farmyard was the mother cat with her five bold and frisky little black and white kittens. In a flash, the mother cat was beside her shy kitten, licking her all over with a warm red tongue.

"Where have you been?" she cried. "We're all ready to start on a picnic."

The picnic was for all the farmyard animals.
There were seeds for the chickens, water bugs
for the ducks, and carrots and cabbages for the
rabbits. There were flies for the frog, and there
was a trough of mash for the pig.

Yum, yum, yum! How good it all was!

After they had finished eating, everyone was just beginning to feel comfortable and drowsy, when suddenly the frog jumped straight into the air, eyes almost popping out of his head.

"Help! Run!" he cried.

The frog made a leap for the brook.

Everyone scrambled after him and tumbled into the water.

"What is it?" asked the shy little kitten.

"A bee!" groaned the frog. "I bit a bee!"

Then they saw that one side of his mouth was puffed up like a green balloon.

Everybody laughed. They couldn't help it.
Even the frog laughed. They all looked so funny
as they climbed out of the brook.

The shy little kitten stood off to one side. She felt so good that she turned a backward somersault, right there in the long meadow grass. "This is the best day ever," said the shy little kitten.